Not Yet!

Written by Megan Borgert-Spaniol

Illustrated by Jeff Crowther

GRL Consultants, Diane Craig and Monica Marx, Certified Literacy Specialists

Lerner Publications ◆ Minneapolis

Note from a GRL Consultant
This Pull Ahead leveled book has been carefully designed for beginning readers.
A team of guided reading literacy experts has reviewed and leveled the book to
ensure readers pull ahead and experience success.

Lerner Publications Company
An imprint of Lerner Publishing Group, Inc.
241 First Avenue North
Minneapolis, MN 55401 USA

For reading levels and more information, look up this title at www.lernerbooks.com.

Main body text set in Mikado 24/41
Typeface provided by Hannes von Doehren.

The images in this book are used with the permission of: Jeff Crowther

Library of Congress Cataloging-in-Publication Data

Names: Borgert-Spaniol, Megan, 1989- author. | Crowther, Jeff, illustrator.
Title: Not yet! / Megan Borgert-Spaniol, Jeff Crowther.
Description: Minneapolis, MN : Lerner Publications, [2022] | Series: Be a good sport (pull ahead readers people smarts - fiction) | Includes index. | Audience: Ages 4–7 | Audience: Grades K–1 | Summary: "Malik is counting for hide-and-seek. Nia wants to go before he counts to ten, but Malik tells her to wait and follow the rules. Pairs with the nonfiction title Following the Rules"— Provided by publisher.
Identifiers: LCCN 2021010315 (print) | LCCN 2021010316 (ebook) | ISBN 9781728441009 (library binding) | ISBN 9781728444376 (ebook)
Subjects: LCSH: Sportsmanship—Juvenile literature. | Hide-and-seek—Juvenile literature.
Classification: LCC GV706.3 .B674 2022 (print) | LCC GV706.3 (ebook) | DDC 796.1/4—dc23

LC record available at https://lccn.loc.gov/2021010315
LC ebook record available at https://lccn.loc.gov/2021010316

Manufactured in the United States of America
1 – CG – 12/15/21

Table of Contents

Not Yet!

The kids played
hide-and-seek.
"We'll count to ten,"
said Malik.
"I will hide," said Zoe.

"One, two, three,"
Malik said.

"Can we go now?"
asked Nia.
"Not yet!" said Malik.

"Four, five, six," Malik said.

"Can we go now?"
asked Nia.

"Not yet!" said Malik.

"Seven, eight, nine,"
Malik said.
"Can we go now?"
asked Nia.

"Ten!" Malik said.

"Now we can go!"

Can you think of a time when you followed the rules?

Did You See It?

lamp   sofa   table

Index

16